Chad Gadya

Passover Story

About One Little Goat....

By Rachel Mintz

This is the story about a small little goat.

A little goat my dad had bought.

You will never guess what happened next.

Dad wanted to buy a large goat but all he managed to find in his pockets were two rusty old coins. Only two coins.

Just enough to afford one small skinny goat.

The poor little goat which dad had bought, was out in the yard.

When suddenly into the yard jumped a large ginger cat!

The cat snatched the skinny little goat and ate it!

As it leaped away the cat called to dad and said "I ate your little skinny goat! The one you bought with your two coins... If you like it or not, I am the master of the yard."

As the cat leaped off the fence, one of the dogs overheard what it said.

"No you are not the master of this yard" the dog barked, he jumped from his spot opening his mouth as wide as he could and caught the cat in mid air.

The ginger cat was not fast enough!

The dog gave it a big bite and swallowed it. "I caught the cat which ate the little goat that dad bought with his two rusty coins. I am the strongest one in this yard!"

A wooden stick which was laying near by, heard the dog.

How dare him think he is the strongest one in the yard.. thought the stick.

I am made of the hardest wood, I am thick and fearless.

The stick flipped over and landed in a frisk blow on the dog, knocking it off its feet.

"Ha!" said the stick "This shows everyone who is in charge around here. I knocked the dog which got the cat, which ate the little goat, that dad had bought with his two rusty coins. This makes me the invincible one around here."

The stick kept rolling twice until it fell on the ground. The fire which was at the side of the yard saw everything. How can a stick think it is invincible? though the fire.

It glowed in a bright blaze and sent embers toward the stick.

Within minutes the stick caught fire and burned.

"Let everyone here know, who is the real almighty! I burned the stick which hit the dog, that bit the cat which ate the little goat that dad bought with his rusty two coins."

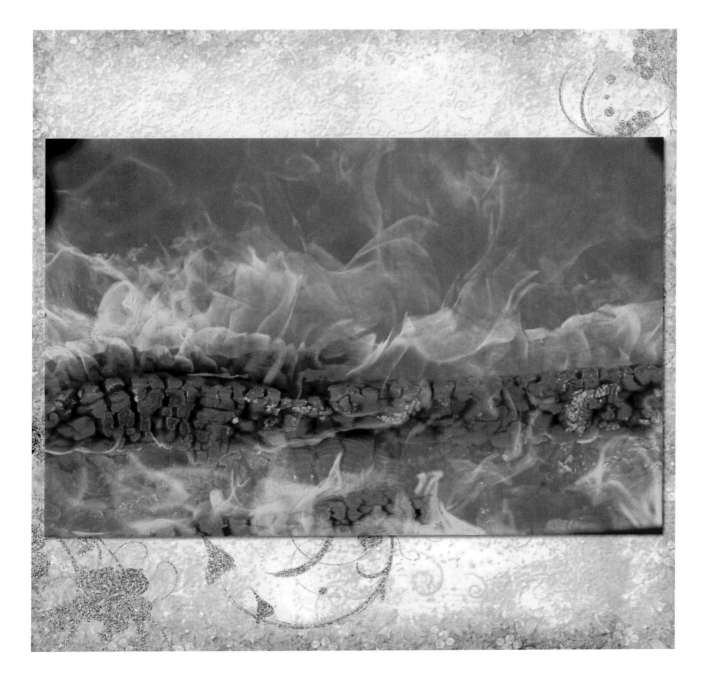

The fire was sure it was the strongest of all the elements. It blazed higher and higher feeling like it owns the place. But then came the water, swaying inside a bucket. The water poured themselves on the fire and the flames disappeared in a silent smoky hiss.

"Who is the strongest one now, ha?" said the water "I extinguished the fire, which burned the stick, which beat the dog that ate the cat that ate the little goat that dad bought with his last two coins. I'm the strongest one of all."

While the water was so pleased to show off how powerful it is, into the yard strolled a large ox. The ox came from a long day in the field and was so very thirsty. It looked around the yard and saw the bucket of water.

It lowered its large head and gulped the water, all the way till the last drop.

"I just drank the water" it burped, "which extinguished the fire, which burned the stick, that beat the dog, that bit the cat, that ate the little goat that dad bought with his last two coins. I guess this makes me the strongest of them all."

But the ox was out of luck.

There was a big celebration planned and many guests were expected to arrive and to be fed. The butcher came to the yard and took the ox to his shop...

Later on that evening the butcher said "I chopped the ox, who drank the water that put out the fire which burned the stick, that smacked the dog, that got the cat, that ate the little goat which dad had bought with his two rusty coins...
In THIS world, there is no doubt, it is the man who is the strongest one of all!"

Up above, the angel of death watched the whole scene from the gates of hell.

He heard what the butcher said.

"What do these pitiful creatures think to themselves?"

"It is I, the angel of death who do as I like, no one is stronger than me" he left his place and soared down to earth with his black long gown.

That night the angel of death killed the butcher.

When he returned to the gates of hell he said "I killed the butcher, which chopped the ox, that drank the water, that put out the fire, that burned the stick, which smacked the dog, that got the cat which ate the little goat that dad bought with his last two coins."

The angel of death was so pleased of himself he shouted "let everyone know,

I am the true almighty of the wo.....!"

He didn't even finish the sentence.

GOD arrived,

and smote the angel of death.

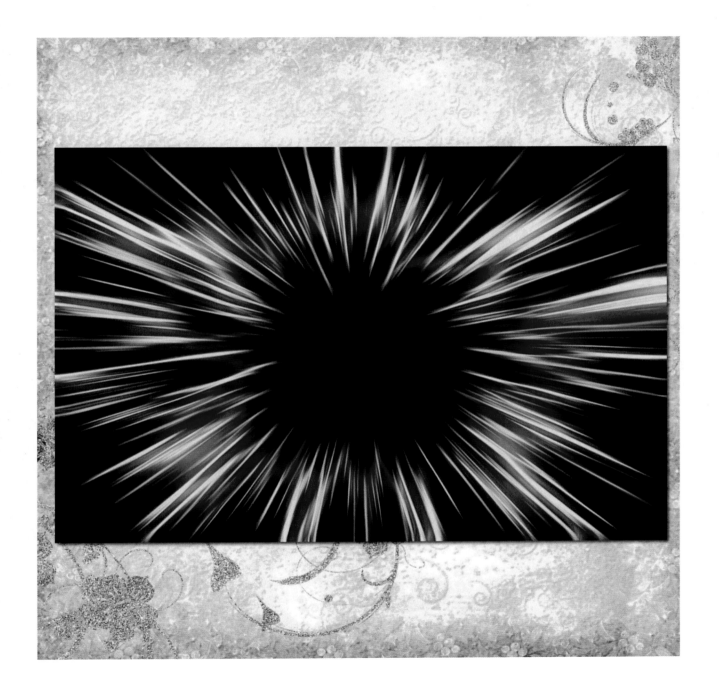

GOD almighty got rid of the angel of death who killed the butcher, who chopped the ox, which drank the water, that extinguished the fire, that burned the stick, that beat the dog, that bit the cat, that ate the little goat which dad had bought with his last two coins.

Now dad had no coins, and no goat.

But he knew one important thing.

He knew who is the one almighty ruler of this world.

The End

More Passover Books For You:

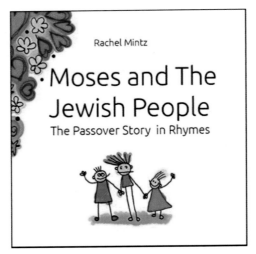

Order Jewish Festivals Fun Books

Hanukkah
Fun Book For Children
Hanukkiah | Dreidel | Latkes | Judah Maccabee
Menorah | Candles | Miracle | Cruse of Oil | Songs
Rachel Mintz & David Levin

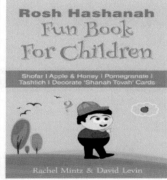
Rosh Hashanah
Fun Book For Children
Shofar | Apple & Honey | Pomegranate |
Tashlich | Decorate 'Shanah Tovah' Cards
Rachel Mintz & David Levin

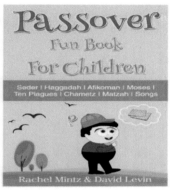
Passover
Fun Book For Children
Seder | Haggadah | Afikoman | Moses |
Ten Plagues | Chametz | Matzah | Songs
Rachel Mintz & David Levin

Purim
Fun Book For Children
Scrolls of Esther | Mordechai | Achashverosh
Mishloach Manot | Shushan | Wicked Haman
Rachel Mintz & David Levin

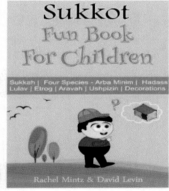
Sukkot
Fun Book For Children
Sukkah | Four Species - Arba Minim | Hadass
Lulav | Etrog | Aravah | Ushpizin | Decorations
Rachel Mintz & David Levin

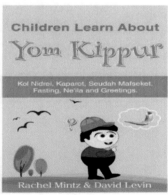
Children Learn About Yom Kippur
Kol Nidrei, Kaparot, Seudah Mafseket,
Fasting, Ne'ila and Greetings.
Rachel Mintz & David Levin

Shavuot
Fun Book For Children
Omer Counting | Harvest Festival | Jerusalem
Chag Matan Torah | Puzzles | Fun Activities
Rachel Mintz & David Levin

Fun way to enrich your kids about more Jewish festivals.
Learning the main themes and traditions for each festival with colorful puzzles and creative activities

Hebrew Counting Books

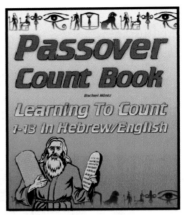

Learning Hebrew Alphabet & Vowels

Learn how to read Hebrew Vowels. The best book to learn Niqqud. For those who know the Hebrew Aleph-Bet.

Improve the kids Hebrew by learning with a coloring book and practice pages.

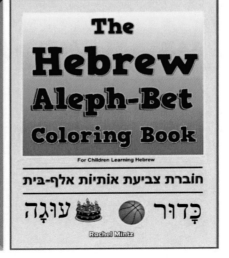

Short Story Books For Kids

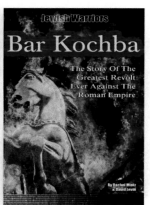

A boy deals with bullies at school like Judah Maccabee.	Passover exodus story with Zombies	The story of the legendary Bar Kochba.

Quick Decoration Kit Books

Sukkot & Hanukkah
Home, Sukkah, Classroom

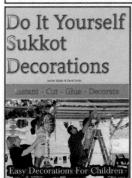

A fun Jewish Tale for Rosh Hashanah

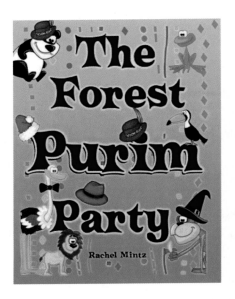

The Forest Purim Party

Rachel Mintz

The Sneaky Tricky Hamantash

A Purim Story

Rachel Mintz

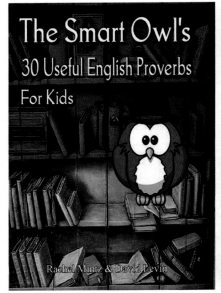

The Smart Owl's
30 Useful English Proverbs
For Kids

Rachel Mintz & David Levin

Piki The Flea
Visits
The Reef

Children Activity Book, Zoom Out From Coral Reef Fish

By Rachel Mintz

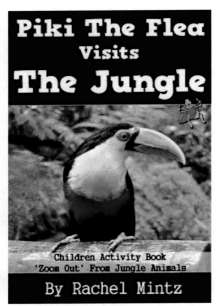

Piki The Flea
Visits
The Jungle

Children Activity Book
'Zoom Out' From Jungle Animals

By Rachel Mintz

Please take a moment to write me a review – Thanks.

Happy Passover

Rachel Mintz

Made in the USA
Las Vegas, NV
18 April 2024

88852856R00024